Me

Lizzie

Grandpa

Pa

Ma

CREAKY OLD HOUSE

A Topsy-Turvy Tale of a Real Fixer-Upper

BY Linda Ashman

ILLUSTRATED BY
Michael Chesworth

STERLING

New York / London

For Betty and Brian, with love
—L. A.

For Adelaide and Calvin
—M. C.

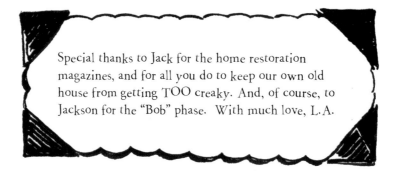

Special thanks to Jack for the home restoration
magazines, and for all you do to keep our own old
house from getting TOO creaky. And, of course, to
Jackson for the "Bob" phase. With much love, L.A.

STERLING and the distinctive Sterling logo are registered trademarks of Sterling Publishing Co., Inc.

Library of Congress Cataloging-in-Publication Data

Ashman, Linda.
Creaky old house / Linda Ashman ; illustrated by Michael Chesworth.
  p. cm.
Summary: A large family gets into an increasingly complicated home repair situation
when the doorknob falls off a door.
ISBN 978-1-4027-4461-7
[1. Stories in rhyme. 2. Dwellings--Maintenance and repair--Fiction.
3. Family life--Fiction.] I. Chesworth, Michael, ill. II. Title.
  PZ8.3.A775Cr 2009
  [E]—dc22

2008037836

2 4 6 8 10 9 7 5 3 1

Published by Sterling Publishing Co., Inc.
387 Park Avenue South, New York, NY 10016
Text copyright © 2009 by Linda Ashman
Illustrations copyright © 2009 by Michael Chesworth
Distributed in Canada by Sterling Publishing
c/o Canadian Manda Group, 165 Dufferin Street
Toronto, Ontario, Canada M6K 3H6
Distributed in the United Kingdom by GMC Distribution Services
Castle Place, 166 High Street, Lewes, East Sussex, England BN7 1XU
Distributed in Australia by Capricorn Link (Australia) Pty. Ltd.
P.O. Box 704, Windsor, NSW 2756, Australia

Printed in China

The artwork for this book was created in ink, watercolor,
and pencil on d'Arches hot-press watercolor paper.

Designed by Judythe Sieck

Sterling ISBN 978-1-4027-4461-7

For information about custom editions, special sales, premium and
corporate purchases, please contact Sterling Special Sales Department
at 800-805-5489 or specialsales@sterlingpublishing.com.

OUR HOUSE is kind of old and creaky.
Porch is sloping, roof is leaky.
Windows drafty, shutters peeling.
There's a crack across the ceiling.
Paint's a little chipped and faded.
Might say it's dilapidated.
Still, each one of us—all nine—
thinks the house is fine, just fine.

We love the yard, the old oak trees,
the favorite spots and memories:

Lou first toddled down this hall.
John drew pictures on that wall.
In the parlor, by the phone,
Pa records how much we've grown.

Here's the quiet corner nook
where Mama goes to read a book.
And the ancient, fraying rug
where Gran and Grandpa jitterbug.

This is where we carved our names,
where Uncle Bob builds model trains,
and the giant claw-foot tub
where Dudley gets his monthly scrub.

Here's the trapdoor Lizzie found,
the banister we all slide down,
the hallway where we like to race...
and my secret hiding place. (Sssshhhhh!)

We love our house in every way—
or did, that is, till yesterday.

Pa was headed out the door
when—CLANG!—the doorknob hit the floor.
"Looks like it needs a screw," he said.
"Bet we've got one in the shed."

We swiped the cobwebs, blew the dust,
tossed a moldy sandwich crust.
Dug through hammers, wrenches, tacks,
cardboard boxes, stacks and stacks.

Searched through buckets, bins, and pails.
Sorted washers, nuts, and nails.
And then, at last, we found a screw.
"Aha!" said Ma. "This one should do!"

We ran inside and down the hall.
"We'll fix it in no time at all!"
But we were wrong . . .

. . . it was too small.

"Uh-oh!" little Lizzie sang.
John said, "Drat!" Lou said, "Dang!"
"Seems to me," drawled Uncle Bob,
"we'd better get another knob."

And so we eyed the knob and door,
then marched to Wally's Hardware Store.
(That's Wally's, built in 1910,
and never cleaned—not once—since then.)

We searched through hinges, levers, latches,
doorstops, doorbells, bolts, and sashes,
brackets, knockers, address plates,
pulls and handles, crates and crates!

We picked through doorknobs: brass and steel,
amber, violet, emerald, teal,
porcelain, crystal, egg-shaped, round—
a knob for every door in town!

Grandpa hollered, "This is it!
We'll fix that doorknob lickety-split."
The trouble was . . .

. . . it didn't fit.

Grandma frowned and shook her head.
"Guess we need a door," she said.

And so our eighteen tired feet
trudged outside and down the street
to Dorothy's Door Emporium,
weighing choices, one by one.

We studied every door design,
considered alder, maple, pine,
mirrored, louvered, painted, leaded,
fancy doors with jewels embedded,
craftsman, cottage, stable, Dutch,
bi-fold, paneled—way too much!

"This should do the trick!" Pa cried.
"Our finest," Dorothy said with pride.
What a shame . . .

...it was too wide.

Nine faces stared in disbelief.
Grandma muttered, "Oh, good grief!"
"Now, now," said Ma. "It's not so bad.
We'll move the doorframe just a tad."

"But then," said John, "the couch won't fit.
We'll have to shift that wall a bit."
"Fine," said Lou, "but if we do,
we'll have to move the stairway, too."

And so it went all afternoon—
we huddled in the living room,
squabbling over building plans,
sketching maps and diagrams,
building models out of blocks,
toothpicks, and a cardboard box.

"Move that bookshelf."

"Bump this wall."

"Shift the den."

"Extend the hall."

"Push the kitchen back a smidge."

At last we had a grand design
that everybody loved, all nine.
We voted to approve . . . but wait!
When hands went up, we counted eight!

Grandma bellowed, "Lizzie's gone!"
"Search the attic!" hollered John.
"And the basement," Lou decreed.
"Everywhere!" we all agreed.

Sixteen legs ran all around—
inside, outside, up and down—

then to the front ... where Lizzie sat,
grinning like the Cheshire Cat.
"Well, I'll be," said Uncle Bob ...

"... Lizzie's gone and fixed that knob!"

Eight faces stared in disbelief.
Sighed Grandma, "What a huge relief!"
"Now it's like it was before."
"Don't need to buy that brand new door."
"Don't need a wider doorframe then."
"Or the bookshelves."
"Or the den."

"Wouldn't need to move that wall."
"Wouldn't need to build at all."
"I never liked that new design."
Said Ma, "Our place is fine, just fine."
"I love it as it is," said Lou.
Grandpa smiled and said, "Me, too."

And so we tore the plans we'd made,
    mixed a batch of lemonade,
        marched across the creaky floor,

out the slightly crooked door,
      settled on the old porch swing
            (a little bent and wobbling) . . .

. . . and didn't change a single thing.

John

Lou

Grandma

Uncle Bob

Dudley